DISCUS THROWING
SLURP!
TOSS!
DAZZLE!
LONG JUMP PIT
HELP!
QUICK SAND
1
2
3

£6-49

The
DENNIS the MENACE
LIPOSUCTION MACHINE
PUFF-PUFF
WHIRR!
GENTLE BUFF
FILE!
MANICURIST'S TABLE

Printed and Published in Great Britain by D. C. THOMSON & CO., LTD.,
185 FLEET STREET, LONDON EC4A 2HS.

ISBN 0-85116-830-2

DENNIS'S
BEACHCOMBING IS GREAT FUN! YOU NEVER KNOW WHAT YOU'LL FIND WASHED UP ON THE BEACH!
BOOT!
COUGH!
LOOK! SOME DRIFTWOOD! FETCH IT, GNASHER!
GNASH! GNASH!
BUT WITH THOSE SOFTY MUSCLES, WALTER DOES LOOK LIKE A STICK! HEE-HEE!
STICK INSECT, GMORE LIKE!
UNHAND ME! ER, UNJAW ME!
THE HORRIBLE HOUND HAS SLOBBERED OFF ALL MY SUN TAN LOTION. BETTER GET SOME MORE FOR MY DELICATE, PORCELAIN SKIN!
OYSTERS CAN BE WASHED UP, TOO. RASHER LIKES OYSTERS.
SLOBBER! SCHLURP!
HOW DISGUST
TOS
WALTER'S MUM

UPPANCE!
ER, THAT'S A BIG LUMP OF WOOD, PAL!
LEMME GO! LEMME GO! SQUEAL! YOU HORRID HOUND!
SNIP!
GNOT ONLY THAT — IT TALKS!
SEA WEED?
WELL, BEA WEED IN THE SEA! HAW-HAW!
UGH! AWFUL SLICK!
ME COULDN'T HELP IT. MUCH!
NOT SWIMMING IN THAT POLLUTION!
PSSS!
PSSS!
WAH!
YOU'LL CHANGE YOUR MIND SOON, WALTER'S MUM.
KICK!
PING!
PING!
SHRIEK!
PING!
PING!
SEE, HE DOESN'T LIKE THE PEARLS INSIDE THE OYSTERS.
SCHLOO!

LOVELY! HE'S GIVEN ME A SUPER PEARL NECKLACE! WHAT A CHARMING PIG!
YOU'LL SOON CHANGE YOUR MIND AGAIN.
CHEWY CHOMP!
TIME FOR A SHOWER WITH THE SPONGE. MIND IF I BORROW YOUR SHOWER GEL, WALTER?
SNATCH!
HEY!
IT ISN'T SHOWER GEL. BUT I DON'T MIND.
WHY NOT?
BECAUSE IT'S SUN TAN OIL! HEE-HEE!
WHAT??? IT'S ALL OVER MY HAIR!!!
ROCK-HARD!
OO! I DON'T LIKE THIS BEACH COMBING.

BLE!
PLUD!
SEE? HE SOMETIMES MAKES MISTAKES — SPITS OUT THE OYSTERS, TOO!
GNEE-HEE!
WHAT'S THIS? A SPONGE!
POUR!
SQUEEZE!
GNNGH! GOTTA GETTIT OUT!
TUG!
'COS IT REALLY, REALLY HURTS! CAREFUL, GNASHER! HOWL! OO!

PET'S THE WAY
TO DO IT!

YAHOO! IT'S 'PETS DAY' AT SCHOOL!
ZOOM!

WHAT A BUNCH OF WIMPS— THEY EVEN LOOK LIKE THEIR PETS!
I DON'T LOOK ANYTHING LIKE MY PET TORTOISE, TANK!
OF COURSE YOU DO!
NO, I DON'T—ERK!
I'LL PROVE IT!
LIFT
I'M S-STUCK!
THAT'S THE IDEA!
WASTE PAPER
SEE? EXACTLY LIKE YOUR PET! HAR-HAR!
BAH!
STUCK.
WASTE PAPER
EVEN YOU LOOK LIKE YOUR PET!
ME? HOW COULD I LOOK LIKE A BIRD?
SHAKE
NERVOUS REX.
TREMBLE
BOOO!
LIKE THAT!
R-ROTTER!
SQUAWK! PRETTY POLLY!
GNEE! GNEE!
ENOUGH IS ENOUGH— I SHALL INFORM HIS FATHER!
TUG!
SOON—
NOW, WHO LOOKS EXACTLY LIKE HIS PETS? SNIGGER!
HO-HO!
SQUAWKEE!
...NNNNG!
TUG! TUG!
SNARL!

HE WHO MUST BE OBEYED!
GLEN
GRAND
PET OBEDIENCE
COMPETITION
TOW
HUH! I HATE QUEUES...
...SHOO!
GRAND
PET OBEDIENCE
COMPETITION
TOWN

IN THE HALL—
VERY OBEDIENT PETS—THEY ALL DID AS THEY WERE TOLD!
SNIGGER!
THAT WAS VERY NAUGHTY! JUST FOR THAT, MY FOO-FOO WILL BEAT ALL YOUR PETS!
OH, YEAH? WHAT CAN FOO-FOO DO?
DAZED
FOO-FOO'S VERY GOOD AT 'ROLLING OVER'—SHOW HIM, FOO-FOO!
HUH! EVEN RASHER CAN DO THAT!
ROLL
EEEEK!
ROLL OVER, RASHER!
TUMBLE
ROLL
SQUISH
CRUMBS! FOO-FOO'S REALLY GOOD AT 'PLAYING SICK'!
SNIVEL!
GASP! WHEEZE!
NOW, WATCH THIS. GNASHER AND GNIPPER—'BEHIND'!
THAT'S WRONG—YOU SHOULD SAY 'HEEL'!
I KNOW WHAT I MEANT TO SAY!
OOO-OOYAH!
BITE
COMPLAIN! COMPLAIN!
DON'T WORRY, WALTER—DENNIS'S PETS WILL FIND THE NAUGHTY LAD!
SO—
IT'S LUCKY MY PETS AREN'T OBEDIENT!
SEEK DENNIS!
POINT
POINT

EGG-STREME MENACING
WE'RE OFF TO ROLL OUR HARD-BOILED EASTER EGGS.
HUH! I'D RATHER...
... ROLL SOFT-BOILED EASTER MUGS!
EEEK!
THROW
THUD!
THUMP!
ROLL
OOOYAH!

I CAN HAVE FUN ROLLING OTHER KINDS OF FOOD THOUGH!
PLOP!
FRIDGE
MY OLD CARTIE WILL DO FOR TRANSPORT!
READER'S VOICE
THAT'S NO GOOD– IT DOESN'T HAVE WHEELS!
IT DOES NOW– FROZEN PIZZAS!
GNASHEE!
TRUNDLE!
ZOOM!
FIRST, I'LL ROLL DAD'S SPECIAL EXTRA-STRONG, SMELLY CHEESE.
HUM
GNERK!
OH, DEAR! THE SOFTIES HAVE SWOONED!
SWOON
THROW
TRUNDLE!
I'LL HAVE TO WAKEN THEM UP AGAIN! I'LL ROLL THESE!
Z-Z-Z
ROLL!
ROLL!
SUCH FUN!
SPLUTTER!
BUMP!
FIZZZ!
BUMP!
BUMP!
ERK! SUCH FUN MUST STOP– RUN AWAY!
WHERE'S MY CHEESE?
SUNK! MY WHEELS HAVE DEFROSTED!
FLOP
FLOP
FLOP
BUT YOUR ASSETS ARE FROZEN!
ULP! WH-WHAT DOES THAT MEAN?
GRAB
IT MEANS NO POCKET-MONEY UNTIL YOU PAY FOR ALL THIS FOOD!
GROAN! ROLL ON SUMMER!
TEE-HEE!
SHAKE

DENNIS and the DINMAKERS
MUSICAL MAYHEM
HIP HOP
OLD FOLK'S HOME
HIP REPLACEMENT GROUP
GENTLE TWANGING
HOP
TAP! TAP!
SPIN!
SWISH!
BUMP!
WHEEEE!
THUD!
CLAP!
HOP!

GNASHER AND GNIPPER
GNUH! OUR COLLARS ARE WORN, GNIPPER!
GNEED GNEW ONES, DAD!
Gnext —
CHURCH SUPPLIES
PET SHOP
WRONG SHOP, DAD!
GNOW WHAT I'M DOING!
GNICE DOG COLLARS, ARE THEY GNOT?
GNUH? REVEREND GNASHER AND GNIPPER!
GNICE TO SEE YOU!
GNAHA! WE CAN DO THE VICAR STUFF, TOO, SON!
GNEAT IDEA!
SWING!

PUT PEGS ON OUR GNOSES FIRST!
BEA'S ROOM
BEA'S NAPPY!
UGH! CHOKE!
PUTRID PONG!
PUKE!
HORRID
SPLOOOSH!
REMEMBER TO WET THE BABY'S HEAD!
SQUIRT!
DONE IT!
GNOW TIME FOR A WEDDING!
DOH!
WAARGH! WAARGH! FLEEING, THAT'S WHAT I'M DOING!
SO!
GNHAW-HAW-HAW!
GNHO-HO!
BARRY GLENNARD
GNEEK! COLLARED!
GOT YOU, GOOD GUYS!
YANK!

GNEE-HEE!
AARGH!
WE DO CHRISTENINGS NEXT.
SCREAM!
PLACE BABY GENTLY IN THE FONT!
SPLOT!
GNO PROB!
WHO HAS THE RING?
EH? WHAT? WHAT AM I DOING IN THIS FIELD?
YOU'VE GOT THE RING, BULLY? PUT IT ON, WALTER!
EEK! WHAT AM I DOING IN THIS FIELD — WITH MY FINGER IN A BULL'S NOSE?
YOU KNOW, THERE'S ANOTHER THING US VICARS DO.
GNULP! FUNERALS?
GNO — WORSE, GNIPPER!
OH, FOR THE WINGS OF A DOVE!
CHOIR SINGING! GNOT FAIR!
OO! SOUNDS LIKE A HERD OF CATS!

WHAT A BUMMER!
COLLECT GNASHER AND GNIPPER'S DOGGY-BICS FROM THE SHOPS, DENNIS!
OK, MUM!
ZOOM!
NOT A SNIGGER, READERS–I'M WARNING YOU!
SHAKE
SIZZLE!
SILENT MIRTH

LUCKY YOU'VE GOT MORE THAN ONE PAIR. NOW COLLECT THOSE DOGGY-BICS!
OK, MUM!
SO—
THIS'LL BE QUICKER!
TRUNDLE
WE'LL COME TOO!
ERK! YOU'LL HAVE ME...
GRAB
LEAP
ZOOM!
...OWWWWT!
TOPPLE
SCRAPE
ZOOM!
NOW SEE WHAT YOU'VE DONE!
SIZZLE
THAT'S YOUR LAST PAIR—BE CAREFUL!
THEY'RE JUST NOT STRONG ENOUGH!
I'LL GET THE DOGGY-BICS!
AND I'LL KEEP THE DOGS AND YOUR TROUSERS SAFE!
GRAB
LATER—
WHERE ARE THE DOGGY-BICS?
IN MY...
ZOOM!
...BACK POCKETS!
THERE'S ONLY ONE THING GOING TO BE STRONG ENOUGH FOR YOUR TROUSERS!
RIP!
ENOUGH FOR TWO PAIRS!
GREAT!
NOT ONE SNIGGER— OR ELSE!
ZIP!
ZIP!

KEEP IT UP, DENNIS

I'M TRYING TO KEEP THE BALL OFF THE GROUND AS LONG AS I CAN!
THUD!
THUD!
GRRREAT!
BOUNCE!
BOUNCE!
KICK!
KICK!
BOUNCE!

MAYBE I COULD DO A LITTLE MENACING AS WELL!
BUS STOP
THUD! THUD!
BOOMFF!
SWOOSH!
HOWL!
THUMP!
GLUB!
BUS STOP
I KNEW THERE WOULD BE WATER IN THERE AFTER THE RAIN!
WE'LL TELL YOUR DAD!
THUD!
THUD!
OOPS! THAT WINDOW'S BROKEN UNLESS— WALTER, COOEE!
SLICE!
THEN—
WHO CALLS?
SMACK!
THUD!
THUD!
MMPH!
NICE 'HEADER'— OR SHOULD I SAY— 'FACER', WALTER!
OOPS! GONE SLIGHTLY OFF COURSE, BUT THE BALL'S STILL OFF THE GROUND!
THUD! THUD!
LEAP
NOW I'M TRYING TO KEEP ME OFF THE GROUND AS LONG AS I CAN!
WHEW! REACHED IT!
KICK!
STOMP!
MY FACE! MY FLOWERS!
THUD!
THUD!
GURRR!

GAME FOR A LAUGH
TRA-LA-LAH...
EEK!
EEK!
SNATCH!
TRUNDLE!
STOP WHINING, WALTER— IT'S NOT OFTEN YOU GET TO PLAY GAMES WITH ME!
SOB! SOB!
LEAP
JUMP
LEAP

B-BUT I D-DON'T LIKE PLAYING THESE ROUGH GAMES!
OK—WE'LL PLAY SOMETHING YOU LIKE...
UNTIE
... LIKE SKIPPING!
OOOH, LOVELY! I LOVE SKIP...
... NNNNGGG!...
... BUT NOT THAT FAST!
WHAT A MOANER!
I'LL GET YOU OUT, THOUGH!
WHIP
BUMP!
OOOH!
I LIKE NICE GAMES—LIKE 'THE FARMER'S IN HIS DEN'!
I CAN PLAY THAT!
STAMP!
THE FARMER'S IN...
WHIRRR!
ZOOM!
... HIS...
LET GO!
LET GO!
HOWL!
... STY! SORRY—I DON'T HAVE A FARMER'S 'DEN', WALTER!
H-HOW H-H-HORRID!
SQUELCH!
AT DENNIS'S DAD'S HOUSE—
MUMBLE! MUMBLE! COMPLAIN!
IT'S 'CHASE AND CATCH' NOW, BUT I DON'T THINK DAD'S PLAYING!
ZOOM!

What have I done . . .
Went shopping. Wahey!
THE JACOBITE
62005
Crossed swords with some Scottish Menaces!
Gave some pals a shower!

Ate a pie or twenty.
Generously GAVE a pie to the Beano Ed.
...to deserve THIS!
Kissy - kissy!
You handsome Menace, you!

YOU'VE BEEN FLAMED!

I'M GOING TO BE A FIREMAN AND ANSWER ALL THE EMERGENCY CALLS!
FIRE STATION
HELP! MUMSIE!
ZOOM!
LEAP
MEE-MAW! MEE-MAW!
FIRE
SQUEAL OF TYRES

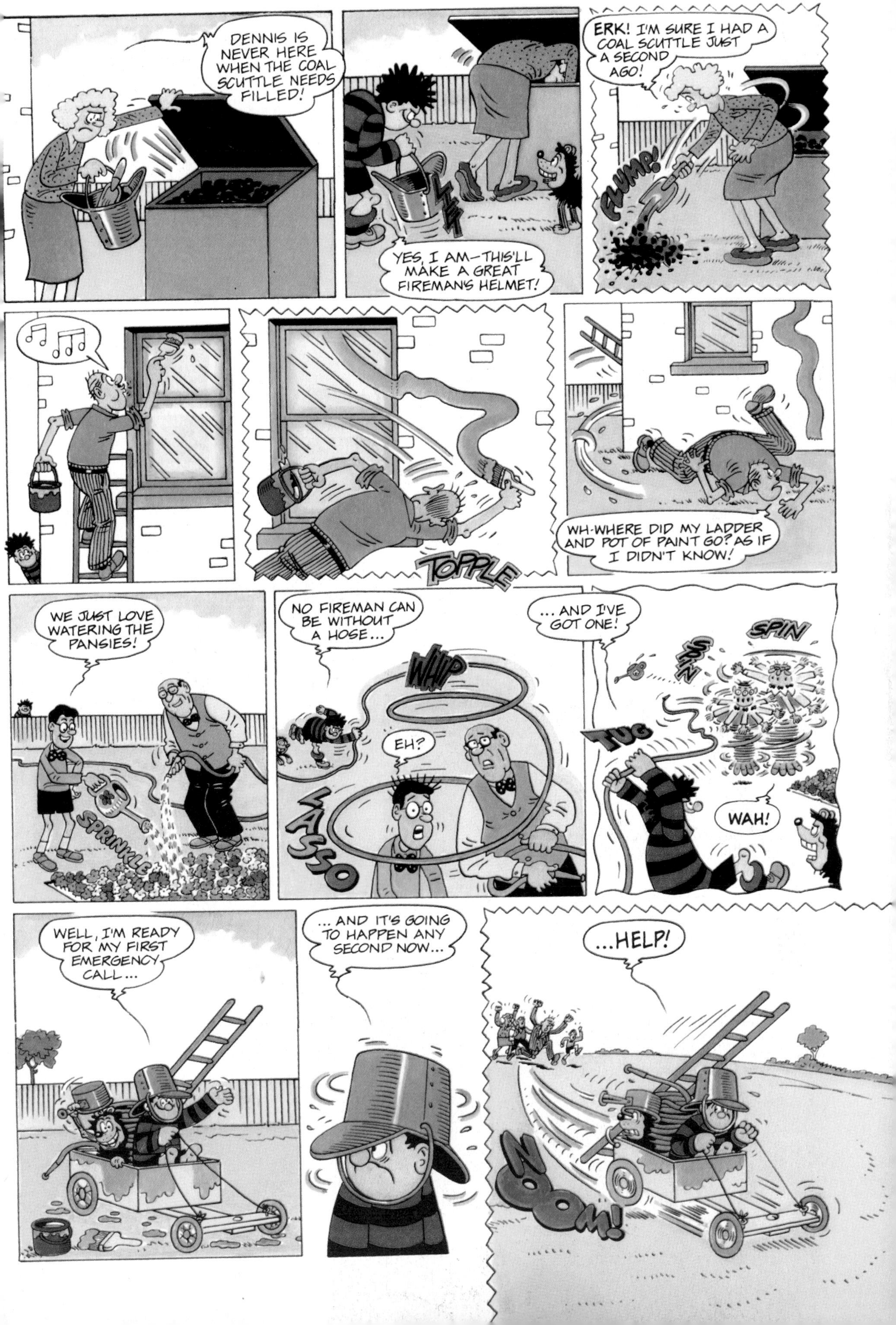
DENNIS IS NEVER HERE WHEN THE COAL SCUTTLE NEEDS FILLED!
YES, I AM—THIS'LL MAKE A GREAT FIREMAN'S HELMET!
ERK! I'M SURE I HAD A COAL SCUTTLE JUST A SECOND AGO!
FLUMP!
TOPPLE
WH-WHERE DID MY LADDER AND POT OF PAINT GO? AS IF I DIDN'T KNOW!
WE JUST LOVE WATERING THE PANSIES!
SPRINKLE
NO FIREMAN CAN BE WITHOUT A HOSE...
WHIP
EH?
LASSO
...AND I'VE GOT ONE!
SPIN
SPIN
TUG
WAH!
WELL, I'M READY FOR MY FIRST EMERGENCY CALL...
...AND IT'S GOING TO HAPPEN ANY SECOND NOW...
...HELP!
NOOM!

'WOOD' YOU BELIEVE IT?
GO UP TO THE SAWMILL AND COLLECT OUR FIREWOOD!
GNZZZZ!
HMPH!
AT THE SAWMILL—
HELP YOURSELF!
SAWM
OH, BOY!
SAWMILL
YAHOOOO!
I DIDN'T MEAN TO HELP YOURSELF TO THAT!
RUMBLE!
RUMBLE!

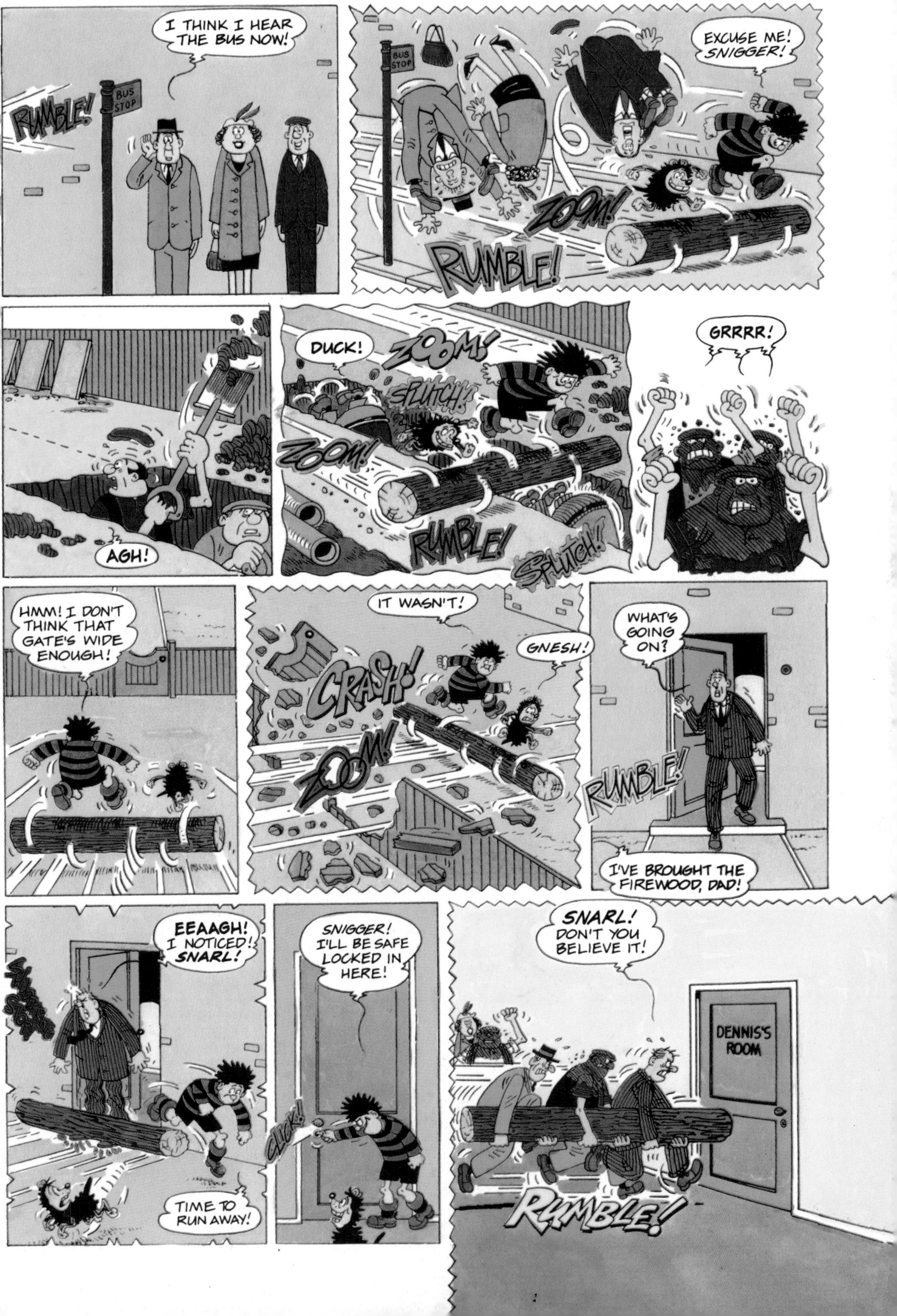
I THINK I HEAR THE BUS NOW!
RUMBLE!
BUS STOP
BUS STOP
EXCUSE ME! SNIGGER!
ZOOM!
RUMBLE!
AGH!
DUCK!
ZOOM!
SPLUTCH!
ZOOM!
RUMBLE!
SPLUTCH!
GRRRR!
HMM! I DON'T THINK THAT GATE'S WIDE ENOUGH!
IT WASN'T!
GNESH!
CRASH!
ZOOM!
WHAT'S GOING ON?
RUMBLE!
I'VE BROUGHT THE FIREWOOD, DAD!
EEAAGH! I NOTICED! SNARL!
TIME TO RUN AWAY!
SNIGGER! I'LL BE SAFE LOCKED IN HERE!
CLICK!
SNARL! DON'T YOU BELIEVE IT!
DENNIS'S ROOM
RUMBLE!

DENNIS and the DINMAKERS
MUSICAL MAYHEM
GARAGE
AIR GUITAR
FREE AIR
TWANG!
SPLUTCH!
CRASH!
BLAST!
OIL
BOING -DA- BOING!
TOOLS
OIL
OIL

BEA IN SISTER DOIN' IT FOR HERSELF!
Apologies to The Eurythmics! Bea loves 'Sisters are doing it for themselves'!
OH, DEAR! BET BEA SINGS ALONG WITH THAT C.D.!
ME LOVES DIS DITTY!
EURYTHMICS
NIGEL PARKINSON
She does!
NOW DER WOZ A TIME, DEY USED TA SAY, DAT BEHIND EVERY GREAT MAN —
WHAT?
— DERE 'AD TO BE A GREAT WOMAN. BUT IN DESE TIMES A' CHANGE, DAT'S NO LONGER TROO.
LET ME HELP.
SO WE'S COMIN' OUTTA DA KITCHEN, 'COS DERE'S SOMEFING WE FORGOT TA SAY TA YOU . . .
BAM!
Chorus!
SISTER IS DOIN' IT FOR HERSELF! STANDIN' ON HER OWN TOO FEET —
HOWL! MY TOOTSIES!
STOMP!

AN' RINGIN' ON HER OWN BELL!
SISTER IS DOIN' IT FOR HERSELF!
MY TIE! NOT A BELL ROPE! GLERK!
SECOND VERSE NOW, PALS. READY FOR IT?
NOW DIS ISSA SONG TA CELEBRATE, DA CONSHUS LIBRARATION OF DA FEMALE STATE. MUMMYS, DAUGHTERS AN DERE DAUGHTERS, TOO. WOOMAN TA WOOMAN, ME'S SINGIN' TA YOU. DA INFERIOR LOT GOTTA NEW EXTERIOR. WE GOT DOCTORS, LAWYERS, POLLYTISHANS, TOO. EVERYBODY, TAKE A PEEP AROUN'. CAN YA SEE, CAN YA SEE DERE'S A WOMAN RITE NEXT TO YOO!
SISTERS IS DOIN' IT FER THEMSELVES!
AN' RINGIN' ON DERE OWN BELLS!
GLERK!
THANK GOODNESS THEY'VE GONE!

BRAVO, BEA, BRAVO!
GREAT SONG, SISTER!
JOIN IN, DEN, SISTERS!
HOWL! OUR TOES!
AARGH!
TOOTSIE PAIN!
STANDIN' ON DERE OWN TOO FEET . . .
STOMP!
CLOG!
STAMP!
HOOF!
SISTERS IS DOING' IT FOR THEMSELVES. STANDIN' ON DERE OWN TOO FEET, AN' RINGIN' ON DERE OWN BELL!
WHO'D WANT A SISTER LIKE THEM?
EH? WHAT WAS THAT? DID I MISS SOMETHING?
DOH!

THE DEFECTIVE DETECTIVE
HM! THERE'S A BURGLAR BREAKING INTO HOUSES AROUND HERE!
THERE IS?
DAILY BLAH
DO YOU MIND?
THERE IS!
DAILY BLAH
COME, FAITHFUL HOUND— WE'LL SOON CAPTURE THE VILLAIN!
PLOD! PLOD!
SNIFF!

VERY SUSPICIOUS—WE COULD BE ON TO SOMETHING, MY DEAR GNASHER!
SNIFF!
THERE'S THE BADDY—ELEMENTARY, MY DEAR GNASHER!
PULL, MY DEAR GNASHER!
GRAB
GRIP
POP!
POP!
POP!
POP!
POP!
TUG
TUG
CRASH!
ULP! I FEAR WE MUST LOOK ELSEWHERE FOR OUR BURGLAR. THIS IS AN HONEST CITIZEN, IN FACT HE LIVES HERE!
BURBLE!
NO MISTAKE THIS TIME! THAT'S MR POTTS' GARDEN!
SNIP!
SNIP!
MY MAGNIFYING GLASS WILL COME IN USEFUL!
SIZZZLE!
BURN
ULP! AND THAT'S MR POTTS—HE WAS JUST TRIMMING HIS PRIZE BUSH! MY MISTAKE!
TOPPLE!
SNIP!
OOOOOHYAH!
GURRR!
RAGE
COME, MY DEAR GNASHER—WE KNOW WHEN WE'RE NOT WANTED!
DRAG
WANTED
WANTED
OOER—MY MISTAKE AGAIN—WE ARE WANTED!

GROUNDED FORCE!
YAHOO!
JUST OFF TO PLAY, MUM!
ZOOM!
THUD! THUD!
NO, YOU'RE NOT— YOU'RE BEING KEPT IN FOR BEING BAD!
PUSH
SLAM SHUT
BAH! FOILED!
SPLAT!
ZOOOOOOM!
SPLAT!
HEH! HEH!
TAP! TAP!

IT WON'T STOP ME HAVING FUN, THOUGH!
RIGHT— PULL!
GRAB
PING!
TWANG!
PYOING!
A FEW NAILS...
TUG
TUG
... AND OUR CARTIE RUN'S READY!
ZOOOOM!
YAHOO!
RUMBLE!
WONDER IF DENNIS IS BEING GOOD?
BLAM!
LIFT
ZOOOM!
THUD!
CRASH!
CRUMBS! YOU'RE IN TROUBLE NOW, DENNIS!
YES, I KNOW...
...I'M NOT SUPPOSED TO BE OUTSIDE!
MY CARPET! MY DOOR! MY FENCE!
STOMP

The Teddy Bears and
HAVE A KNOB OF SALT-FREE BUTTER!
HOW THOUGHTFUL OF YOU!
HAR-HAR! THE TEDDY BEARS ARE HAVING A PICNIC!
MAY I HAVE SOME SQUASH?
POUR
CERTAINLY, WALTER, IT WILL HELP WASH DOWN YOUR PATÉ!
BUM BAG
EXTRA POP

Teddy Boys Picnic
I DO SO LIKE A CHICKEN DRUMSTICK.
MY AUNTS! KISSY-WISSY!
MWAH! MWAH!
KISS!
FOR HANDIES
TOOFY PICKS
Turn over for — THE TEDDY BOYS' PICNIC!

The Teddy Bears an
CRASH!
SHRIEK!
BOOMF!
HAVE ANUVVER 'BUTTER'! HAW-HAW!
LEAP!
WHEEE!
ZOOM!
PAT!
SPLURT!
YOU'LL NEED A WASH AFTER SOME COW PATE!

eddy Boys Picnic
I'M GNASHING GREAT WITH DRUMSTICKS!
SQUEAL!
SQUASH!
SPLASH!
SCRATCH!
EEK!
KISS THESE ANTS, AUNTS!
SCRATCH!
SCRATCH!

WOULDN'T IT BE GLOVELY?

GNULP!
BEANO
BEANO

I'M GOING TO GET EVER SO FIT AND BASH DENNIS. TITTER!
EEK!
SCREECH TO A HALT!
B-BUT N-NOT TODAY!
KICK
HOI!
CEMENT
ZOOM!
SLITHER
WHAT A LOVELY DAY!
THUD!
OW!
THUNK!
THAT WAS YOUR FAULT!
NO, IT WAS HIS!
B-BUT I'VE GOT AN EXCUSE...
LOOK!
SOON—
... DISGRACE, ALLOWING THE MENACE OUT WITH BOXING GLOVES!
WHAT ARE YOU TALKING ABOUT?
YES!
HE WAS JUST COLLECTING A TIN OF HIS FAVOURITE TOFFEES FOR HIS GRAN'S BIRTHDAY!
AND ROTTEN MUM TIED THESE GLOVES ON ME SO I COULDN'T GET IN THE TIN!
ERK!
FUMBLE
TOFFEE

CAMPING ROUGH!
WHAT'S THIS? A SPONSORED WALK?
NO...
... WE'RE ALL GOING TO COMPLAIN ABOUT THE MENACE!
AND THEY'RE NOT GETTING IN— I'VE TURNED THIS PLACE INTO AN ARMY CAMP!
GNESHOO!
GURR!
SNARL!
WATER
SOOT BOMBS
PEAS
INK PELLETS
CAMP MENACE
ENTER AT YOUR OWN RISK!

WHAT'S THE PASSWORD?
WE'VE COME TO COMPLAIN...
WRONG PASSWORD!
RUN AWAY! RUN AWAY!
SNIGGER! NEXT!
WHAT'S THE PASSWORD?
IT'S ABOUT YOUR DOGS AND I'M NOT SCARED OF THAT OLD DRAIN-PIPE EITHER—SO THERE!
WRONG PASSWORD AS WELL!
SOOT
S-SOOT BOMBS ARE A DIFFERENT MATTER—NOW THEY SCARE ME!
COMPLAIN, COMPLAIN!
HMMM...
I'LL PUT A STOP TO THIS!
BUT HOW? YOU DON'T KNOW THE PASSWORD EITHER!
WHAT'S THE PASSWORD?
PEAS
NO POCKET MONEY—EVER—UNLESS I GET IN NOW!
ULP! TH-THAT'S C-CLOSE ENOUGH TO THE REAL PASSWORD!
HUH! THE C.O.'S PUT ME IN THE GUARDHOUSE FOR A WEEK!
GNASHER
TEE-HEE!
SNIGGER!

DENNIS and the DINMAKERS
MUSICAL MAYHEM
The BLUES
SWOOSH!
SWOOSH!
BLUEBERRY JUICE
SKIP!
SKIP!
SKIP!

ACT YOUR AGE
IF I WAS YOUR AGE —
YES, GRANNY?
— I'D BE OUT CLUBBING! STRUTTING MY STUFF.
WIGGLE
CLICK!
GRANNY . . .
. . . YOU DO THAT ANYWAY!
NIGHT CLUB
MUSIC
DANCING
DISCO
OH, YES. SO I DO. HEE-HEE!
BUT OTHER OLD FOLK AREN'T LIKE MY GRANNY. THEY ACT THEIR AGE. DOING OLD FOLK'S STUFF. LIKE GARDENING, READING, BOWLING, BALLROOM DANCING, GROWING GREY HAIR. ALL THAT STUFF.
ZONK
TUG
SLIP
CRUNCH
BUT WHEN I'M THAT AGE, GUESS HOW I'LL ACT! TURN THE PAGE TO FIND OUT, READERS.

ENGLAND
BOWLING
STRIKE! I LOVE BOWLING!
CLICK!
CLICK!
CLICK!
EEK! NOT THAT KIND OF BOWLING, DENNIS!
GARDENING
GOING GREY
WAG, GNASHER! ALL OVER WALTER'S WIG!
WIG SHOP
NEW WIG
WAG! WAG!
GREY

BALL ROOM
ROOM FOR ONE MORE BALL?
'RESCUED' FROM BEANOTOWN MUSEUM
BOOM!
SHRIEK!
WAHEY! I'LL CUT YOUR GRASS — WITH MY COMBINE HARVESTER!
CRASH!
BALLROOM DANCING
READING
I LIKE TO GET MY FEET UP TO DO A SPOT OF READING!
FLATTEN
BUMP!
VROOM
CRUNCH

GYM'LL FIX IT!
WAH!
GYM TEACHER
AS YOU CAN SEE DENNIS IS GOOD AT GYM...
... IN FACT, HE'S THE SCHOOL CHAMPION!
BOINNG!
BOINNNG!

WHAT A SILLY PLACE TO STAND!
GYM TEACHER
P-PRACTISE TILL I GET BACK!
WAVE
I C-CAN'T CLIMB THIS — IT'S T-TOO HIGH!
OF COURSE YOU CAN! I'LL HELP...
PROD
GET UP THAT ROPE!
VROOM!
THUD!
OW!
SEE? YOU NEVER KNOW WHAT YOU CAN DO TILL YOU TRY!
WELL, I CAN'T VAULT THE HORSE, ANYWAY!
SHAKE
GNASHER!
ALL YOU NEEDED WAS A LITTLE PERSUASION!
GNASH! GNASH!
WAH!
BOING!
LEAP
LEAP
SOON—
WELL, I'M NO LONGER SCHOOL GYM CHAMP, BUT I'M NOT BOTHERED...
... BECAUSE I'VE GOT A NEW JOB TILL THE GYM-TEACHER'S BETTER!
TAP
GYM TEACHER
GYM CUP
COO, THANKS!

ART ATTACK!
HUH! THE WRITER'S HEAD'S IN A BUCKET. HE HASN'T BEEN ABLE TO THINK UP A STORY FOR ME TO DRAW!
THINK! THINK! THINK!
'DENNIS the MENACE' ARTIST
DO SOMETHING DRAMATIC SO I CAN DRAW IT, DENNIS!
SOMETHING DRAMATIC? WHAT ABOUT THE LONG JUMP?
SCRATCH
LEAP
PTCHEEEEE!

KERASH!
GROAN! TH-THAT JUMP WAS T-TOO LONG!
SORRY, BUT I'VE ANOTHER IDEA! TO THE SWIMMING POOL!
AT THE SWIMMING BATHS.
I'LL JUMP OFF AND YOU CAN DRAW ME ON THE WAY DOWN.
THAT SOUNDS LIKE A GOOD DRAMATIC PICTURE!
PYOING!
SPLUNGE!
I WAS ST-STANDING T-TOO CLOSE!
SORRY AGAIN! I KNOW— I'LL GET MY CARTIE!
FLOP
GREAT! JUST HOLD THAT POSE!
HEY...
... YOU FORGOT TO DRAW BRAKES ON MY CARTIE!
DAZED
SNEEZE! I'M TOO ILL TO DRAW— YOU'LL HAVE TO FINISH THE STORY YOURSELF!
WHAT WOULD MAKE A GOOD DRAMATIC PICTURE?
THIS IS ALL YOUR FAULT!
WHAP!
KICK
UNCLE AL, THE KIDDIES PAL

OH, WHAT A CIRCUS!
COME ON, GNASHER. WE HAVE WORK TO DO!
SWISH
CIRCUS
GNASH! GNASH!
CIRCUS
EEK!
HAR! HAR! ROUNDING UP AN AUDIENCE FOR OUR 'CIRCUS'!
SWISH
YEOWL!
CRACK!
THWACK!

BRING ON THE BIG CATS!
EH? DON'T SEE ANY CAGES!
CRACK
CRACK
GNIP!
GNASH!
MEOW!
SCREECH!
HA-HA! LIKE TO GIVE THE AUDIENCE A CLOSE UP VIEW OF THE ACTS!
NEXT...
WAH!
...THE BEARDED LADY! TA-RA!
TUG
ZZZZZ
MUM
WOW!
THEN-
EEK! WHERE'D ALL THESE PEOPLE COME FROM? HELP!
AND-
HUH! CHEAT!
HELP!
GNEEK!
GNIPPER
AHEM! AND A SPECTACULAR FEAT TO FINISH!
SO-
EH? DENNIS AS A PAINTED FACED CLOWN! NOT MUCH OF A GRAND FINISH!
GROAN! NOT A CLOWN! THOUGHT I'D PUT MY HEAD INTO RASHER'S OPEN MOUTH! GAG! GAG!
BOILK! BURP!
HA-HA-HA!
CHORTLE!
VERY BRAVE!
HOW DARING!
CLAP
WILT
TOPPLE
GNEEK! CAN'T HOLD DENNIS MUCH LONGER!
NNNG!

DENNIS, BEA, MUM, DAD, GNASHER AND RASHER
IN... "OH, BRUVVER!"
SHUCKS! YOU'RE TOO KIND, LITTLE SIS.
ME LOVES BIG BRUVVER.
NIGEL PARKINSON
ER — WHAT DOES THE WINNER GET?
A BIG CASH PRIZE.
£3.76 ALL IN PENNIES.
WAS £100 NOW £3.76
HMM!
MUM'S BEST CHINA CABINET
WE'RE HAVING THE GRAND NATIONAL.

NOT YOU, DENNIS — BIG BRUVVER ONNA TELLY.
SHE MEANS WHEN PEOPLE GET VOTED OUT OF THE HOUSE ONE BY ONE.
LET'S TRY IT. CURLY AN' PIE-FACE CAN BE JUDGES.
SHOPPING! SHOPPING! I'M OFF SHOPPING!
SHE'S TAKEN MY PENNIES — THAT'S ONE OUTTA DE HOUSE!
Soon —
WE'LL SHOW THE JUDGES OUR MENACING ABILITIES.
THIS HOUSE MATE'S GOING TO HAVE TO REPAIR THAT HOLE.
AND GNASHERNAL, MORE LIKE. TEE-HEE-HEE!
MAGNIFICENT MENACING!
JAM
TERRIFIC MESS!

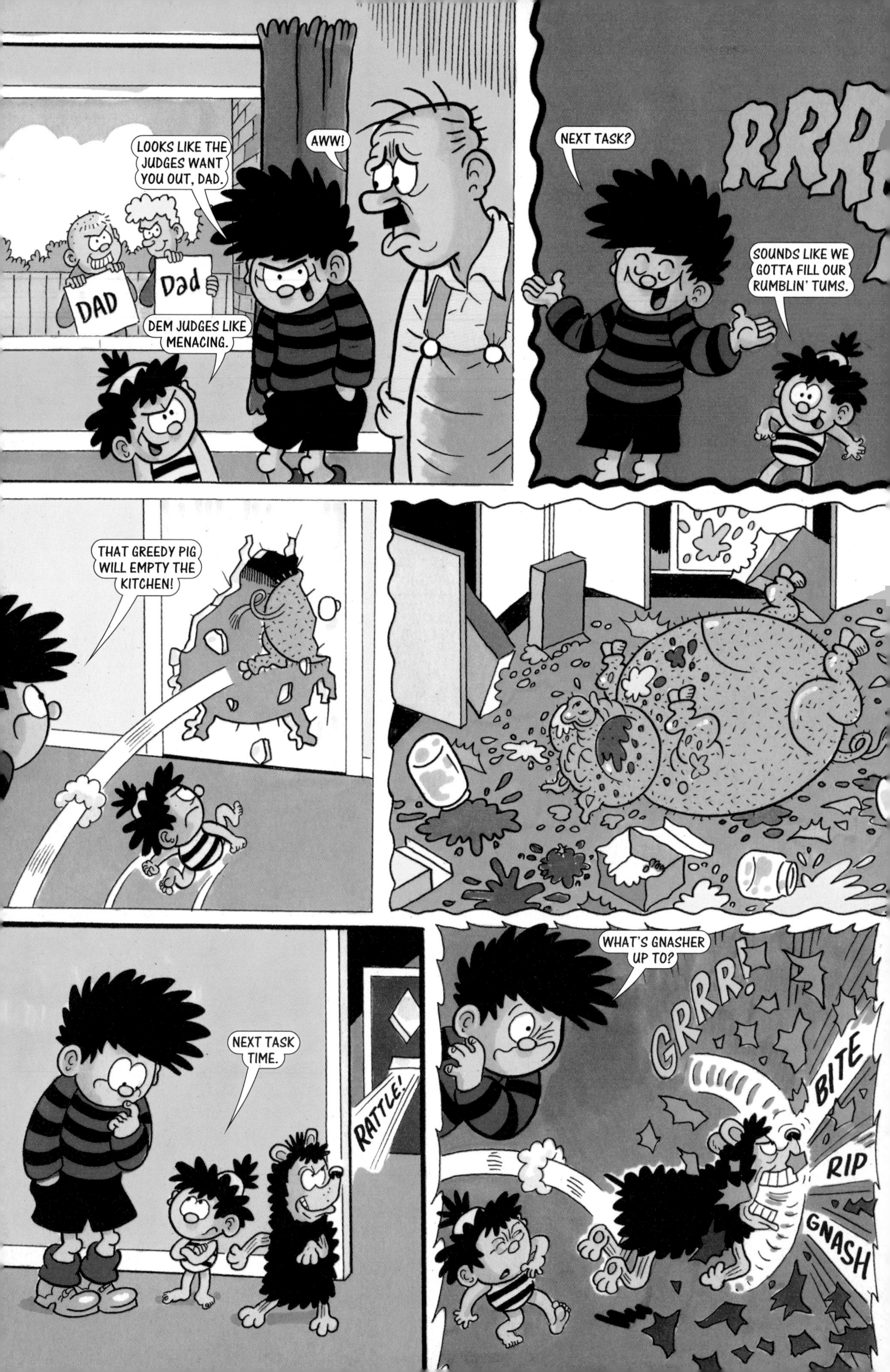

LOOKS LIKE THE JUDGES WANT YOU OUT, DAD.
AWW!
DAD
Dad
DEM JUDGES LIKE MENACING.
NEXT TASK?
RRR
SOUNDS LIKE WE GOTTA FILL OUR RUMBLIN' TUMS.
THAT GREEDY PIG WILL EMPTY THE KITCHEN!
NEXT TASK TIME.
RATTLE!
WHAT'S GNASHER UP TO?
GRRR!
BITE
RIP
GNASH

GANGWAY!
WASN'T OUR TUMS RUMBLIN'! WAS RASHER'S TROTTERS.
RUMBLE
RUMBLE
RUMBLE
RUMBLE
GREEDY-GUTS. HE JUST LEFT THIS FUNNY VEGETABLE FOR ME.
RASHER'S OUT FOR BEING SO GREEDY.
ONLY THREE LEFT.
RASHER
Rasher
WHO CARES? I'M DELIGHTFULLY FULL.
WADDLE
OO-ER! WHAT WAS THAT FOR?
HAR-HAR-HAR!
DON'T YOU THINK THAT "GNASHING THE POSTMAN" WOULD MAKE A GOOD TASK?
IT LOOKS LIKE THE JUDGES DON'T THINK SO!
GNASHER
Gnasher
AW, WELL! IT WAS FUN ANYWAY!
TWO LEFT — WHO'LL WIN?

WORRA FAB MENACE, DENNIS!
. . . ME!
DENNIS
Dennis
SHOCKER! ME'S WON!
WE HAD TO PUT YOU OUT OF THE HOUSE, DENNIS.
BUT, WHY?

YOU IS THE BESTEST MENACE EVER. I'M SURE TO BE VOTED OUT NOW.
RUMBLE
GULP! THINK WE'D BETTER CHANGE OUR VOTES, CURLY.
AND THE LAST PERSON TO BE VOTED OUT IS . . .
NONE OF US WILL EVER GET BACK IN THERE AGAIN!
WASN'T SAFE FOR YOU IN THERE, OLD MATE.
FRRRAAAAP!
NOXIOUS NIFF
PHEW! THANKS, LADS! MUST'VE BEEN THAT CHILLI ME WAS EATIN'!
PUTRID PONG
FRIIIP!
FRRRAWWWP!
UGH! NAPPY WHIFF!

BRACE YOURSELF!
PYOING!
MUM! HAVE YOU SEEN...
... MY BRACES? OOPS!
NO! AND A TOWEL IS MISSING FROM MY WASHING LINE!
WAHEY! THE HIGH FLYING MENACE TODAY!
BOINNNG!
GNEE-HEE!

KEEP GOING, GNASHER!
ZOOM!
PYOING!
BOO!
BEANOTOWN PRISON
PYOING!
THE MENACE!
GASP! THOUGHT WE WERE SAFE IN HERE!
SAVE US!
HAR-HAR! BUNCH OF SOFTIES!
NEXT—
FORWARD, GNASHER!
AND—
HOI!
HO-HO! HIGH CLASS MENACING! BITE! CHOMP!
THEN—
FED UP PUSHING, GNASHER? WANT A TURN TO MENACE?
GNASH! GNASH!
PYOING!
AT WALTER'S HOUSE—
GO MENACE WALTER, GNASHER.
GNBYE!
PYOING!
BUT ON THE OTHER SIDE OF THE FENCE!
GNEEK!
SQUEAL!
SWEET
SMELLY
SPLASH!
WAA! SORRY, GNASHER! HELP!
TEE-HEE!
PERFUME
HOPE GNASHER ENJOYED MY LOVELY BATH WATER!
GNASH! GNASH!
PYOING! PYOING! PYOING!
CRASH!
VERY SWEET SMELL

COP THiS!
SOMEONE'S GOING TO BE MENACED—
OO...ER!
IN THE POLICE STATION—
WHAT'S DENNIS DOING HERE?
GNEEK!
HEH! THE MENACE HAS ARRIVED!
SWOOSH!
SWOOSH!
GLUG!
WIFE'S SHOPPING LIST
WANTED

EH?
CLICK!
CLICK!
WAAAA!
HAR! HAR!
SPIN
HO-HO! THIS'LL COOL YOU DOWN!
BLURB!
SWOOSH!
SNARL! ANYTHING TO SAY BEFORE I DEAL WITH YOU, MENACE!
OOPS! YES...
SNAP!
SNAP!
HAPPY BIRTHDAY TO YOU! HAPPY BIRTHDAY TO YOU! HAPPY BIRTHDAY, SERGEANT JOLLY...
EH? HOW'D YOU KNOW?
HA-HA! BECAUSE YOU'VE JUST HAD A 'MENACE-GRAM'! WE ASKED DENNIS TO DO IT!
GOOD OL' SARGE!
CLAP! CLAP!
CHORTLE!
GREAT FUN! CHOMP!
GNASH! MUNCH!
PHEW! THOUGHT DENNIS HAD GONE BONKERS!

THUMPING GOOD FUN!
CRUNCH!
THUD!
BA-DOOM!
PHEEEEEP!
BRMM!
TEA HUT
TEA UP!
ZOOM!
WAHEY!
GOT THEM OUT OF THE WAY!
SO I COULD BORROW THEIR ROAD THUMPER!
CHUG!
BA-DOOM!
CRACK!
BA-DOOM!
HISS!
SMASH!
BA-DOOM!
CRASH!

BA-DOOM!
HAR-HAR!
YOU!
CRUNCH!
SMASH!
NOW TO...
BA-DOOM!
BA-DOOM!
HOI!
CRUNCH!
... FLATTEN A PHONEBOX! CHORTLE!
THEN—
EEK!
FLATTEN
GREAT FUN!
CRUNCH!
MEN AT WORK
WAH!
BA-DOOM!
BA-DOOM!
VERY SOON—
RANT! COMPLAIN! ABOUT DENNIS! RANT! RANT!
I...I SHALL PUT A STOP TO HIM!
SO—
HMM! I WONDER? NEAR THE SCHOOL HERE!
BASH STREET
HAR-HAR!
SPLAT!
PAINT
BA-DOOM!
THROW
ROLL
SNIGGER!
EH?
BA-CRACK!
HA-HA! I KNEW A CAKE FROM THE BASH STREET COOK'S KITCHEN WOULD BE ENOUGH TO STOP YOU, DENNIS!
HUMPH!
PHUT! PHUT!
AND—
NO POCKET MONEY FOR A MONTH, WASH DISHES FOR A WEEK, BATH TWICE A WEEK...
SNARL!
THUMP!
FLATTEN
THUMP! THUMP! THUMP! THUMP!
HA-HA! DENNIS DOES THE JOB AS GOOD AS THE REAL ROAD THUMPER!

MAYBE I SHOULD'VE BORROWED SOME OTHER ROADWORK GEAR, READERS. LIKE THESE!
MENACES AT WORK
WANNA HAND TO IRON?
CRASH!
SHRIEK!
STEAM ROLLER
PNEUMATIC DRILL
DENTIST
I'LL DRILL YA, WALTER!
DRRRR!
EEK!
OOH! MA . . .

WHIMPER!
SQUEAL!
LINE PAINTER
LINE PAINTING MACHINE
TRAFFIC CONES
LICK!
GNEE-HEE!
TUG!
TEMPORARY TRAFFIC LIGHTS
DISCO LIGHTS, ACTUALLY!
SPIN
PARP!
DRY ICE
HA-HA! WE'RE LAYING LIQUORICE!
HEAT CONTROL
TARMAC LAYING MACHINE
LIQUIFYING TANK
SLOBBER! SCHLURP! DE-LISH!

ROCK-A-BY, SOFTY!
SOPPY LULLABY SOUNDS
WHAT SOPPY NONSENSE IS GOING ON HERE?
PLINK!
PLONK!
ROCK
WALTER THE SOFTY'S DEAR PARENTS
WALTER'S JUST HAVING HIS AFTERNOON NAP! HAR-HAR!
FAINT
SQUEAL! THE MENACE AND HIS HORRID DOG!
PUSH
FAINT
LET'S GO FOR A LITTLE FRESH AIR BEFORE YOUR NAP!
OUR BABY!
OOOH! HELP!
ZOOM!
LEAP

HA-HA!
SPLASH!
ZOOM!
BUT THEN—
RASHER! LOOK OUT!
TRUNDLE
WHEE!
ARGH!
CLANG!
LITTER BIN
CLANG!
OINKEH?
DOH! WHAT ARE YOU WAITING HERE FOR, ANYWAY?
DAZED
LITTER BIN
TAKE AWAY SWILL
SORRY, NO FOIL CONTAINERS AT THE MOMENT!
HMMM!
POINT
SO—
FILL HER UP! HAR-HAR!
EH?
AND!
PERFECT TROUGH! HA-HA!
CHUG!
CHUG!
DROOL!
HA-HA! BREAKFAST IN BED, WALTER!
YEUCH! THIS IS DISGUSTING!
NIFF!
PONG!
ZOOM!
OOPS! TIME FOR US TO TAKE AN AFTERNOON NAP, GNASHER!
MUMMY!
ZOOM!
SO—
POOR LITTLE LAMB!
SNARL! IT'S DANGEROUS TO WAKE SLEEPWALKERS.... BUT WHEN THEY DO WAKE UP—THEY'LL BE FOR IT! GRRR!
ZZZZZZ!
MY LUNCH!
GNZZZZ!

ALL PRESENT-NOT CORRECT!
A LITTLE PRESENT FOR WALTER AND HIS SOFTY CHUMS!
TO YOU, BERTIE!
OO... NOT TOO HARD, WATTIE! I BRUISE SO EASILY!
COTTON WOOL
A PRESENT! SQUEAL!
CLAP!
HOW SPIFFING!
GNASH! GNASH! GNASH!
OOF!
HAR-HAR! IT'S MY—'GNASH IN THE BOX.'
PYOING!
YIKES!

CHOMP! GREAT FUN!
GNASH! GNASH!
EEK!
SCREAM!
UNTIL—
BACK YOU GO, GNASHER! INTO THE BOX!
PUSH
CHOMP! GNASH!
SOON—
Restaurant
NO DOGS OR GNASHER
OKAY! HE'S NOT HERE!
IN THE RESTAURANT—
MAY I TAKE YOUR —AHEM, BOX, SIR?
GENTLE CHOMP!
OKAY!
EEK!
WAA! A GNASHER IN THE BOX!
PYOING!
GNASH! GNASH!
CHOMP!
'GNASH IN THE BOX' STRIKES AGAIN! CHEW!
FLEE!
EEK!
CHOMP! GNASH!
LET'S GO, GNASHER!
ZOOM!
LATER—
HUH! HAVE TO STOP THIS MENACING TRICK FOR A WHILE...
... GNASHER'S EATEN TOO MUCH! HE'S NOW— STUCK IN THE BOX!
GNNNNGH!
HAR-HAR!
HO! HO!
STRAIN
PULL
HEAVE
HEE-HEE!

DRESSED TO THRILL
EVEN THE MENACE HAS TO TAKE CARE WHEN FEEDING PETS! HAR! HAR!
GNIPPER
GNASHER
RASHER
STEEL WOOL GLOVES
SPLATTER
YIKES!
SPLATTER
RASHER
GNEH?
TRIP
NO... STOP! WAA!
MUNCH!
GNASH!
GUZZLE!
LEAP
LEAP
GNIPPER
GNASHER
RASHER

HUMPH! CAN'T GO TO WORK IN THIS!
I CAN'T GO SHOPPING!
ULP!
SO—
OFF TO WORK!
WAVE
HA-HA!
I'LL BE THE LAUGHING STOCK OF THE BUS-STOP, DENNIS!
SIGH!
BUS STOP
EEK!
WAA! A MENACE!
I'LL WALK!
TOWN
BUS STOP
HA-HA! CLEARED THE QUEUE FOR HIM!
BRRM! BRRM!
SUPERMA
THIS'LL TAKE AGES. VERY BUSY!
A MENACE!
SPECIAL TODAY
BEST BUY
HIDE!
STAY AWAY!
SOON—
SUPERMARKET
GREAT! NO BOTHER TODAY!
PHEW! LOOKS AS IF WE'RE GOING TO ESCAPE PUNISHMENT!
BUT LATER—
WELL, WE ARE BEING PUNISHED! AFTER ALL...
HAR-HAR! GOT YOU, DENNIS!
...THREE MENACES IN THE SAME HOUSE IS JUST A LITTLE TOO MUCH! OW! OUCH!
TAKE THAT, DENNIS!
SPLAT!
PONG
BLOW
PONG
SPLAT!
NASTY NIFF
PONG
PONG
STINK BOMBS
STINK BOMB
STINK BOMB
SIGH! HOW CHILDISH!

DENNIS and the DINMAKERS
MUSICAL MAYHEM
NEW WAVE
BLAST!
WHOOSH!
PLEASANT THOUGHTS!

DENNIS and GNASHER
are
ALL AT SEA
EEK!
WAHEY!

WE'RE HAVING A HOLIDAY AT THE SEA-SIDE! SOME GREAT MENACING STUFF HERE.
I'M HERE, TOO. AND I SHALL INFORM YOUR FATHER OF YOUR NAUGHTY, NAUGHTY PLANS.
GH'MM . . !
SOFTY SQUEALER!
PADDLE
ACTUALLY, I DON'T THINK YOU'LL SAY ANYTHING, WALTER!
WHY EVER NOT?
DIVE
'COS YOU WOULDN'T LEAVE THE WATER WITHOUT ANY TRUNKS ON!
SQUEAL! MY WATER WEAR! YOU AWFUL ANIMAL!
GNEE-HEE!
SWOOSH

YOU NAUGHTY TRUNKS-TAKERS! I CAN'T COME OUT OF THE WATER!
THIS ISN'T A SWIMMING MASK.
IT'S A SEA WEED-FLINGING CATAPULT! HA-HA!
TWANG!
WHEE!
'ELLO, WIMPS! HAVE SOME SAND FOR YOUR CASTLE!
NASTY BULLY!
KICK!
SPLAT!
TEMPER TANTRUM
WHO DID THAT? WHO DID THAT? EH? WHO? WHO? WHO DID DO IT?
SNIGGER!
TEMPER TANTRUM
THUD!
STOMP!

COOL DOWN, MATE!
SHAKE!
TUG!
NIP!
NIP!
YEEOWLL!
HA-HA!
SNARL! WAIT TILL I GET YOU!
HO-HO! NO CHANCE, BALDY!
ZOOM!
GOTCHA NOW! YOU CAN'T GET AWAY NOW.
OO-ER!
NO WORRIES! THESE LIMPETS WILL HELP!
STICK!
STICK!
STICK!
TOSS!
GNUH?

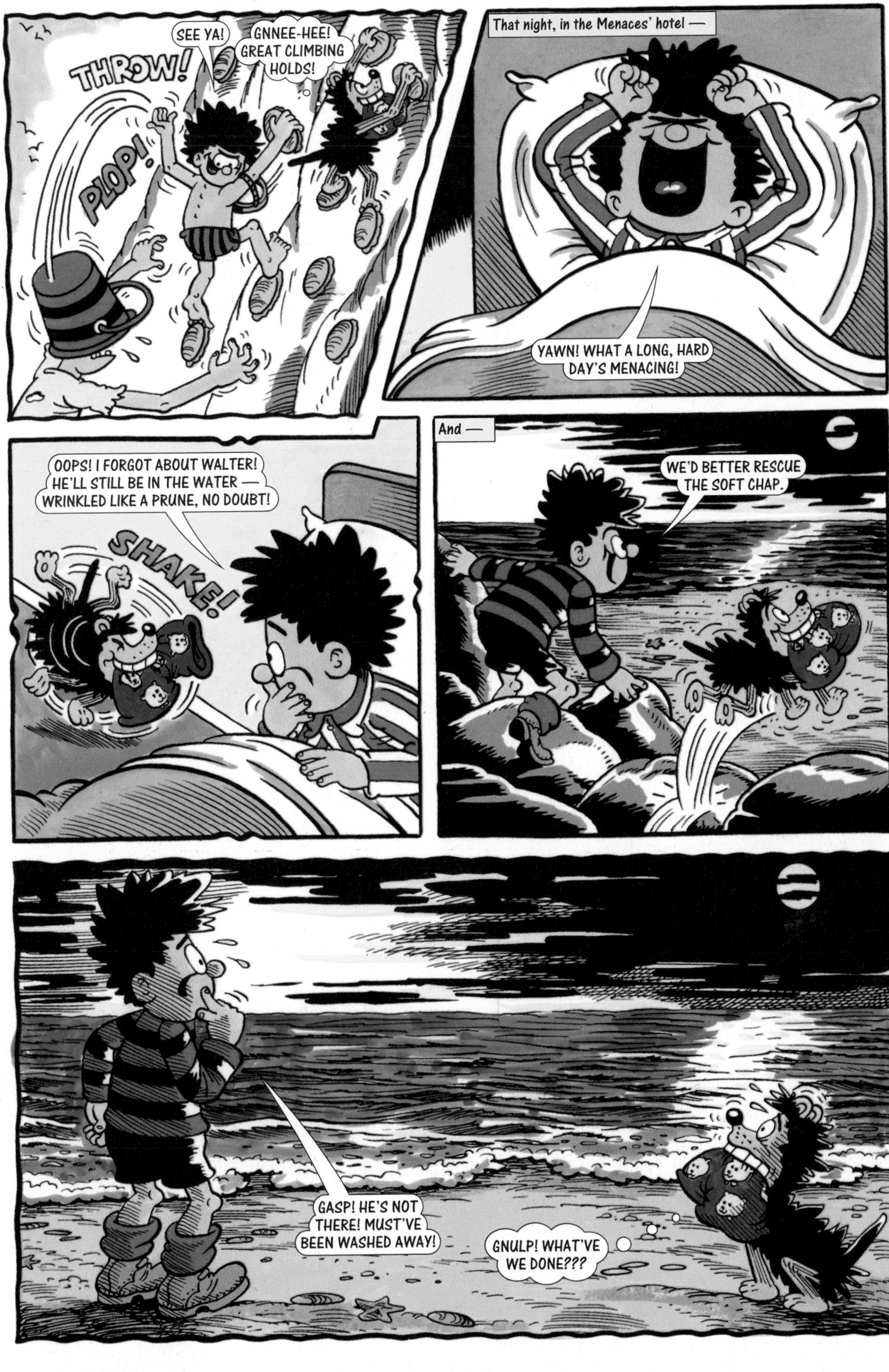
SEE YA!
GNNEE-HEE! GREAT CLIMBING HOLDS!
THROW!
PLOP!
That night, in the Menaces' hotel —
YAWN! WHAT A LONG, HARD DAY'S MENACING!
OOPS! I FORGOT ABOUT WALTER! HE'LL STILL BE IN THE WATER — WRINKLED LIKE A PRUNE, NO DOUBT!
SHAKE!
And —
WE'D BETTER RESCUE THE SOFT CHAP.
GASP! HE'S NOT THERE! MUST'VE BEEN WASHED AWAY!
GNULP! WHAT'VE WE DONE???

But —
DON'T WORRY, SOFTY FANS — I'M SAFELY TUCKED UP IN BEDDY-BYES IN MY JIM-JAMS! CUDDLED UP WITH TEDDY.
TRA-LAA-LAA!
SKIP!
HOW? EASY. I KNITTED MYSELF A PAIR OF NATTY NEW TRUNKS FROM SEA SHELLS AND SEA WEED! TEE-HEE-HEE!
CLICK!
CLICK!

DENNIS and the DINMAKERS
MUSICAL MAYHEM
ROCK
POUND!
THUD!
WHAP!
SCREECH!
TWANG!
GNASH!
BEANO ROCK
CHOMP!
CRUNCH!

Sir Menace Quite-A-Lot!
CLANG!
CLANG!
CLUNK!
BANG!
Dennis's Shed
WHAT'S THE MENACE UP TO NOW?
NEVER FEAR— SIR MENACE IS HERE!
ZOOM!
OH!
GASP!
CRUMP!
SLURP!
GNASH! GNASH!

AHA! A DRAGON, PERHAPS!
GNEH?
CHORTLE! NO! JUST A BIT TOO MUCH CURRY POWDER!
SSSS!
COUGH!
WHOOSH!
INDIAN TAKE AWAY
MENU
VERY HOT
COUGH!
HISSSSSSSSS!
SWOOSH!
SQUIRT!
THANKS, SIR MENACE.
ALL IN A DAY'S—I MEAN KNIGHTS—NO—DAY'S—ER, WORK!
OOH!
HELP!
SQUEAL!
AHA! A DAMSEL IN DISTRESS! FORSOOTH!
IN WALTER'S GARDEN—
HOLD STILL, LITTLE LAMB! MUST GET THE HEM STRAIGHT!
WALTER'S MUMMYKINS
NOT QUITE A DAMSEL IN DISTRESS—BUT CLOSE ENOUGH! HA-HA-HA!
SQUEAL! SHRIEK! WATCH THAT NEEDLE!
EEK!
R-RIP!
SAVED, FAIR MAIDEN! HAR-HAR!
LIFT
MY DRESS!
HAR-HAR! BE QUIET, DAMSEL! I'M TRYING TO RESCUE YOU!
EEEEK! SQUEAL!
SWING
EH? WHAT'S GOING ON? CAN'T GO FORWARDS!
PULL
PULL
C'MERE, SIR MENACE!
PULL
WAAA!
MAGNET
WHIZZ!
CLANG!
AND—
TITTER! EVERY LAST ONE TO BE PICKED UP AS PUNISHMENT, SIR MENACE!
HUMPH! NEVER HAPPENED TO THE KNIGHTS OF THE ROUND TABLE, I'LL BET!
STAB
JAB
SLURP!

SNOW FUN
WELL, IT IS, ACTUALLY!
HUH! MENACES ARE TOUGH! WE DON'T FEEL THE COLD—UNLIKE THE SOFTIES! HA-HA!
OO... YOU MUSTN'T BE COLD, MY LAMBIKINS!
NO, MUMSIE!
GNASH!
I'M AN EXPERT 'SNOWBALLER'! WATCH, GNASHER!
SWISH!
PTCHEEEE!
EXPERT? WHAT A MISS!
THUNK!
SHAKE
SHAKE
SHAKE
AN EXPERT! HOW ELSE CAN YOU SOAK THREE SOFTIES WITH ONE SNOWBALL? HA-HA-HA!
SWISH!
PTCHEEEE!
AAA!
FLUMP!
FLUMP!
FLUMP!
HOW CRUEL!
OO!

AAAARGH!
SPLAT!
A WELL-PLACED SNOWBALL...
THROW
GNASHEE!
BEANOTOWN BAKERY
...CAN BRING YOU HOT BUNS! HA-HA!
SNARL! THE MENACE!
TAKE THAT, MENACE!
HA-HA! WE SURE WILL!
THROW
SNATCH
GNULP!
WATCH ME STOP TIME, GNASHER!
GNEH?
DONG!
DONG!
WHAP!
WHAP!
THE SOFTIES CHALET
STAY OUT, ROUGH BOYS!
GNAH-HA!
DONG!
DING!
SPING!
SPONG!
PYONNG!
EEK!
WAH!
FLUMPFF!
HA-HA! TEN O'CLOCK ALL DAY NOW, GNASHER!
BUT THEN—
SPLAT!
SPLAT!
SPLAT!
SPLAT!
SNOWBALL FIGHT, NOW?
READER!
ULP! NO! GETTING A DISGUISE READY! HOPE THEY DON'T SPOT A 'SNOWBOY AND SNOWDOG'!
DON'T WORRY, SOFT ONES—I'LL TRACK THEM DOWN!
SOB!
SIMPER!
GNEESH!

Good Den Menacelas!
SING ALONG TO THE TUNE OF "GOOD KING WENCESLAS".
GOOD OLD DENNIS ONCE LOOKED IN, ON A FEAST FOR WALTER!
TEE-HEE! I'LL EAT THIS ALL MYSELF!
"SHARE WITH ME, YOU WEEDY SAP, OR YOUR FACE I'LL ALTER!"
WHIMPER!
MOAN!

LOUDLY HOWLED THE SOFTY BOY,
"YOU'RE SO MEAN AND CRUEL".
DENNIS MEANWHILE STUFFED HIS EARS
FULL OF COTTON WOO-OO-OOL!
PLUCK
HOWL!
"BRING ME TURKEY, BRING ME SPUDS,
PEAS, SPROUTS AND TOMATAS.
WHILE YOU'RE AT IT, GIVE'S A FEW
OF THESE CHIPOLATAS!"
VERY SOON HE HAD A PLATE PILED UP LIKE A MOUNTAIN,
MEANWHILE WALTER LOUDLY SOBBED—
TEARS WELLED LIKE A FOU-OUNTAIN!
SLURP!
SOB!
SOB!
"HITHER, GNASHER, STAND BY ME,
BRING OUR GIFT FOR WATTIE.
WE MUST STOP HIS DREADFUL DIN,
OR I'LL GO QUITE POTTY!"
CHOMP!
FOR WALTER
LEAP
WALTER RIPPED THE WRAPPING OFF.
"OO! A LOVELY DOLLY!"
CHOMP! CHEW!
THEN HE SQUEEZED HIS PREZZIE TIGHT—
WHAT AN ACT OF FO-OLLY!
HOWL!
HOPE YOU GET ALL THE PRESENTS YOU WANT, READERS!
GNAPPY GRRISTMAS!
SQUIRT
HUG
SQUEEZE

DENNIS and the DINMAKERS
MUSICAL MAYHEM
R'N'B
RUPERT N BASIL
PERFUME EMPORIUM
SHOCKWAVE!
BLAST!
CLUNK!
CLONK!
THUD!
PERFUME PONG
RNB
SMASH!
CRASH!
RNB
SCENTED NIFF
SHATTER!

OH, DEAR! HOW CAN I STOP BEA CRYING?
WAAH! WAIL! HOWL! SOB!
YOU CAN READ HER OUR ANNUAL!
A Crying Shame!
OR MY ANNUAL!
DENNIS THE MENACE ANNUAL
LET HER LOOK AT THE BEANO WEBSITE — www.beanotown.com
LET HER JOIN THE BEANO CLUB!
BUT IT'D BE QUICKER TO STOP HER EATING THE ONIONS IN YOUR SHOPPING, DAD! HAW-HAW!
WAAH! STINGIN'!
CHOMP!

THE SOFTY OLYMPIC GATHERING
QUIET ZONE
ZZZ
JUDGE'S TENT
SIGN HERE FOR A PRIZE
HOP
CLAP
BATH SALTS
WONDERFUL NIFF!
EXTRA FLOWERS
SPLASH!
SPLASH!
WASHING POST
PERFUME OIL
LOVELY AROMA
BUBBLE BATH